S0-BUB-161

THE MOLE PEOPLE

By
Carl R. Green
and
William R. Sanford

Adapted from a screenplay by
Garrett Fort

Edited by
Dr. Howard Schroeder

Professor in Reading and Language Arts
Dept. of Elementary Education
Mankato State University

Produced and Designed by

BAKER STREET PRODUCTIONS, LTD.

CRESTWOOD HOUSE

Mankato, Minnesota, U.S.A.

7194

LIBRARY OF CONGRESS CATALOGING IN PUBLICATION DATA
Green, Carl R.
The Mole People.

SUMMARY: A team of archeologists digging in the Middle East discovers an underground civilization of mole people.
1. Children's stories, American. (1. Monsters--Fiction. 2. Horror Stories)
I. Sanford, William R. (William Reynolds). II. Schroeder, Howard. III. Title.
PZ7.G8186Mo   1985   (Fic)   84-23913
ISBN 0-89686-262-3 (lib. bdg.)

International Standard Book Number:	Library of Congress Catalog Card Number:
Library Binding 0-89686-262-3	84-23913

With special thanks to Leslie Chang,
who helped get the words right.

Published by:

CRESTWOOD HOUSE
Highway 66 South, P.O. Box 3427
Mankato, MN 56002-3427

TABLE
OF
CONTENTS

■ ■

PROLOGUE

■ ■

Archeologists are scientists who search for the buried past. They seek out the places where ancient people once lived. Then, they dig into the earth, layer-by-layer. If they're lucky, they may find the ruins of a buried city.

Imagine the excitement of digging up a city that no one has seen for thousands of years! What strange secrets lie hidden? Who were the people? How did they live?

Moviemakers have often carried this search a step further. In the movies, archeologists often find a lost civilization — but the people are still alive! They have just been cut off from the rest of the world for a long time. How are the people different? How will they react to modern tools and ideas? Will they be friendly — or dangerous?

These are the questions explored in *The Mole People*. The answers make for an exciting adventure.

1.
THE SEARCH FOR SHARU

Archeologist Roger Bentley wiped the sweat away. The summer was hot in Iraq, but Bentley didn't mind. He knew his "dig" was going well. Still, a bit of cool weather would feel good. The thought made him look toward Kuh-i-Tara, the snowcapped mountain that rose high above the camp.

Just then a running figure caught his eye. It was one of the native workers. The man dodged piles of ancient bricks as he ran. When the native saw Bentley, he waved for the "boss" to follow him. Bentley called to the other scientists and ran after the man.

Some workers were pointing into a newly dug hole. A flat stone was sticking out of the dirt at the bottom of the hole. Bentley told the workers to pull it out.

Scientist Paul Stuart put the heavy stone on a table. The young American brushed off the dirt. "This was lying below that band of clay," he said. "We know the clay was deposited during the Great Flood. That makes this stone over five thousand years old!"

Bentley studied the stone. His voice was calm, as it always was. "It's covered with Sumerian writing.

The archeologists study the stone that tells about Sharu.

Let's see. It tells about a temple built by a king named Sharu. It also says that the Goddess Ishtar will put a curse on anyone who touches this stone."

Etienne LaFarge broke in. He was an older man who had lived in the Middle East for many years.

"I've heard of Sharu before," he said. "His name was on stones found at another dig. Those stones said that Sharu and all his people went away. They were never seen again."

"Okay," Stuart said, "but what about this curse —"

Suddenly, the ground began to shake. Dust rose as the sides of the hole caved in. Then, just as the earthquake ended, the stone of Sharu slid off the table. It fell to the ground and broke into a thousand pieces.

Jud Bellamin picked up one of the pieces. Bellamin was Bentley's chief assistant. He put everyone's thoughts into words. "I don't believe in magic," he said. "But it seems as though Ishtar has punished us for moving that stone."

No one had much to say. The scientists moved off to get the work started again.

That afternoon, a shepherd boy came to Bentley's tent. Bentley gave the boy a coin for the package he carried under his arm. It might be junk, but he had to take the chance. That's the way archeologists worked.

Bentley unwrapped the package. It looked like an old pot, and was covered with mud. As he poked at it, some of the mud broke off. Yellow metal gleamed in the sunlight. It was gold!

"Where did you find this?" he asked the boy.

The boy pointed to Kuh-i-Tara. "Up there," he said.

"That's where the earthquake was centered," LaFarge said. He carefully picked off the rest of the mud. Everyone crowded around the table. It was a beautiful oil lamp.

Bentley found some writing on the side. "I,

Bentley carefully examines the oil lamp.

Sharu, made a home in the ark for my family," he read. "When the flood came, I sailed with my slaves and my animals. We floated until we found the Land of the Snow. It was near the Goddess of Ishtar."

The lamp gave Bentley a great idea. "I know why they were never heard of again!" he said, his eyes blazing. "No one ever looked for Sharu on the top of Kuh-i-Tara. But we will! We'll go on top of the mountain into the wind and snow. That's where we'll find the tomb of Sharu!"

2.
DANGER AT THE
TEMPLE OF ISHTAR

The four archeologists studied the map of Kuh-i-Tara. The climb looked long and dangerous. Bentley turned to Nazar, their native guide. "Tell us about the climb," he said.

"First, we'll set up a base camp where the snow starts," Nazar told them. "Then we can climb up another two thousand feet to that flat area. From there we can push on to the top."

Bellamin wasn't happy about climbing Kuh-i-

10

The archeologists study the map of Mt. Kuh-i-Tara.

Tara. "We're spending a lot of time and money," he said with a frown. "And all because that old lamp has a bit of poetry on it."

Bentley ignored his friend's bad temper. "Remember," he said, "Schliemann found the gold of Troy because he trusted the poetry of Homer." That reminder excited Stuart and LaFarge . The treasure of Troy was one of archeology's greatest finds.

The climb up Kuh-i-Tara started the next morning. A long line of native workers carried the supplies up to the base camp. Above the camp, Bentley could see the first snow fields.

The second day was freezing cold. The wind worked its way through the climbers' heavy clothing. Ice frosted their goggles. The climb was hard and steep. Everyone was tired when they set up camp for the night.

In their tent, the archeologists sat close to a camp stove. "Tomorrow's climb takes us up another three thousand feet," LaFarge reminded them. "The air is thin up there."

"Listen!" said Bentley.

Above the howling wind, they heard a new sound. The noise grew louder and louder and then died away. It was the sound of an avalanche. Bellamin jumped up. He was afraid of being buried alive.

"Relax," Bentley told him. "You'll never hear the avalanche that gets you." Bellamin didn't think that was very funny.

The next morning was clear and cold. Kuh-i-Tara was very steep at this point. The four archeologists roped themselves to Nazar, their guide, and began to climb. An hour later, they heard the thunder of another avalanche.

"Dig in!" Nazar shouted.

The men held tightly to the face of the cliff. Tons of snow and ice roared over their heads. When the avalanche was over, they looked around. The ledge they were on was covered with snow left by the avalanche.

Bellamin was beginning to believe in the curse of Ishtar. "The goddess is still angry at us," he said.

"Maybe not," Bentley said. "Look over there!"

A marble arm stuck up from the snow. "It's part of a statue," Bentley shouted. "The avalanche probably brought it down from the flat area near the top."

The men quickly climbed upward. When they reached the top, they stopped. The sight took their breath away. Before them stood the ruins of an ancient building.

LaFarge was overjoyed. "It's a Sumerian temple," he shouted.

The archeologists walked up the steps of the temple. As they entered, Bellamin found the marble head of a woman. "This is the Goddess Ishtar," he told them. "Remember? The lamp said that Sharu landed near here. Let's set up camp. Then we can begin a proper search."

Paul Stuart was too excited to wait. He walked across the marble floor to look for another statue. Without warning, the floor broke away under him. He screamed as he fell into the darkness under the temple.

3.
TRAPPED IN KUH-I-TARA

Bentley crawled over to the hole and looked down. He couldn't see anything. "Paul!" he called, over and over. Only a faint echo came back from the darkness. He took out a flashlight and snapped it on. The beam showed only the rough sides of the hole.

"We've got to go down," Bentley told the others. LaFarge turned pale, but he agreed to go with his friends.

Nazar begins to lower the party by rope.

Nazar was a good mountain man. He slowly lowered Bentley, Bellamin, and LaFarge into the hole by rope. The hole seemed to go down a long way into the center of the mountain. At the bottom, they found Stuart's body. The American was dead.

Above them, Nazar hammered a metal spike into the side of the hole to hold the rope. His pounding caused a huge stone to break loose. The stone knocked Nazar down as it fell. The guide screamed and tumbled head over heels. He hit the bottom of the hole not far from Bentley, Bellamin, and LaFarge. The men flattened themselves against the side of the hole.

The huge stone had knocked dirt and rocks loose. The avalanche buried the bodies of Stuart and Nazar. When it stopped, the silence was complete. The way back was blocked.

Bentley turned on his flashlight. The beam cut through the blackness. The men saw that they were next to a narrow tunnel. "This isn't a natural cave," Bentley said. "Look at the walls. It was made by something, or someone, alive."

LaFarge was ready to give up. "We're trapped here!" he cried. "We haven't got any food or water!"

Bentley tried to calm him. "There's air coming in. That means there's an opening up ahead. Let's start looking."

As the men started their search, a strange thing happened. First, a small opening appeared in the tunnel wall. Then sharp claws cut a larger hole in the hard earth. Two fiery eyes looked out of the hole. The eyes never blinked as they watched the men. None of the men saw the strange eyes.

Bentley led the way into one dead end after another. The hot air made LaFarge feel sick. He didn't like being so far underground.

Bentley and Bellamin had to help the older man walk. Then, their spirits lifted. They saw a light ahead. They followed the tunnel toward the light.

The route led them into a very large cavern. The light came from glowing rocks in the cavern wall. In the center of the cavern they saw the ruins of another temple. The stones were broken and covered with moss.

Bentley pointed to a fallen statue. "There's another statue of Ishtar! We've found the lost city!" He read the writing on the statue. "I have built this temple for Ishtar with stones from the mountain. Signed, Sharu the Great."

"I guess they escaped the flood," Bentley said. "But then their city fell into the earth during an earthquake. They must have all died down here."

The men decided to lie down for a rest. Close behind them, a handful of dirt fell softly to the ground. Razor-sharp claws reached through a new opening in the wall. LaFarge's head was only a few feet away.

16

Trapped at the bottom of the hole, they find more evidence of the lost city.

17

4.
CAPTIVES IN AN
ANCIENT LAND

LaFarge heard the faint sound of digging. "What was that?" he asked.

"It's probably a bat," Bentley replied. "There's nothing here that can hurt us. Try to get some rest."

The tired scientists were soon asleep. Behind Bentley, the unknown creature worked to make the hole larger. A handful of dirt hit Bentley in the face.

In the next instant, a huge paw covered Bentley's

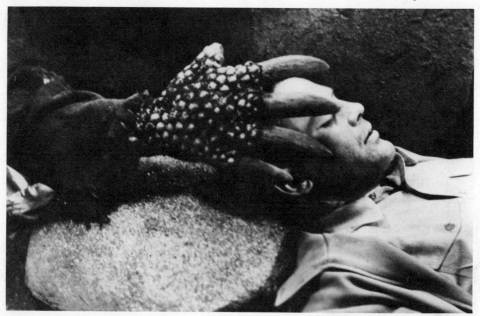

A huge paw closed over Bentley's head.

face. He fought to free himself, but the attacker was too strong. Other creatures pinned Bellamin and LaFarge to the ground. Bellamin felt as though he was wrestling with an alligator.

The silent creatures pulled sacks over the men's head, tied their hands, and led them away. After a long walk, they left their captives in a prison cell.

Bentley was able to free his hands and get the sack off his head. He looked around. This room was lit by glowing rocks, too. In the dim light, Bentley couldn't see a door. Quickly, he helped the others to free themselves. LaFarge was bleeding from five deep scratches on his chest.

"Look at the size of those scratches," Bentley said as he cleaned the wounds. "What were those creatures?"

Nobody could answer his question. Bentley wanted more light. He turned his flashlight on. "They brought us in," Bentley told the others. "There must be a way out. Wait! What's that?"

The flashlight beam lit up a skeleton in the far corner of the room. At first, the skeleton looked human. But the men soon saw that it had long, curved claws instead of fingers. The face was also strange. The eye holes were much larger than those of a human being.

"LaFarge, you're the expert," Bentley said. "What is it?"

LaFarge studied the skeleton. "Well, it walked on

two legs," he told them. "And with those claws, I bet it could dig faster than any mole. It also had a brain as big as yours or mine."

As they studied the skeleton, a door began to open in one of the walls. Strange music floated into the cell. "Don't move!" Bentley commanded. He turned off the flashlight.

Two guards stood outside the door. They carried swords in their hands. Each wore leather armor. In the dim light, Bentley saw that their skin and hair were a milky white.

The guards pointed their swords at the scientists. Bentley nodded, and they all followed the guards. Their route led them toward the music. Soon they could also hear people singing.

The tunnel opened into the large cavern they had seen earlier. Beyond a small stream lay the ruined temple. People sat on a platform near the temple. They were wearing strange clothes, fancier than those of the guards.

Bentley, Bellamin, and LaFarge moved as if they were in a dream. They crossed the stream. The singing stopped as they came closer to the white-skinned people.

"I've studied clothing like that all my life," Bentley said. His usually calm voice shook with excitement. "We've stepped back five thousand years in time. Welcome to ancient Sumer!"

5.
ESCAPE FROM
THE SUMERIANS

The guards led their captives to their ruler. The king wore a high crown and a golden necklace. His eyes were like black marbles.

"Their eyes work best in dim light," Bentley whispered. "Look — no iris and huge pupils."

"There's no sun down here," Bellamin said. "That explains the white hair and skin."

The high priest stood next to the king. Another priest handed him a golden rod. The rod was topped by a slanting arrowhead. Bentley saw the same mark on the guards' uniforms.

The high priest raised the rod. The music stopped at once. Everyone but the king bowed down before the golden rod.

"Hail, King Sharu the Ninety-First! Hail, Sharu, many times great-grandson of Sharu the Great," the high priest sang out. He spoke in the language of ancient Sumer. "I, High Priest Elinu, raise the sacred Eye of Ishtar." Elinu pointed at the three scientists. "These are evil ones. They were captured by the Mole People."

Sharu turned to Elinu. "Their skins are so dark! I've never seen anyone so ugly," he whispered. His

The three captives stand before the king.

cold, black eyes moved back to Bentley. "Who are you?" he asked.

Bentley answered him in Sumerian. "We are friends. We have come from a world far above you."

"Only heaven is above us!" Sharu replied angrily. "And only gods live in heaven. Do you claim to be gods?"

Sharu and Elinu whispered to each other. Then Elinu said, "In the name of Sharu, I say you are evil spirits. You must die in the fire of Ishtar!"

The guards closed in on the captives. Bentley pushed one guard, and Bellamin hit another one. Bellamin grabbed a sword as the three men ran back into the tunnel. A guard jumped in front of them.

Bentley fights with a Sumerian guard.

24

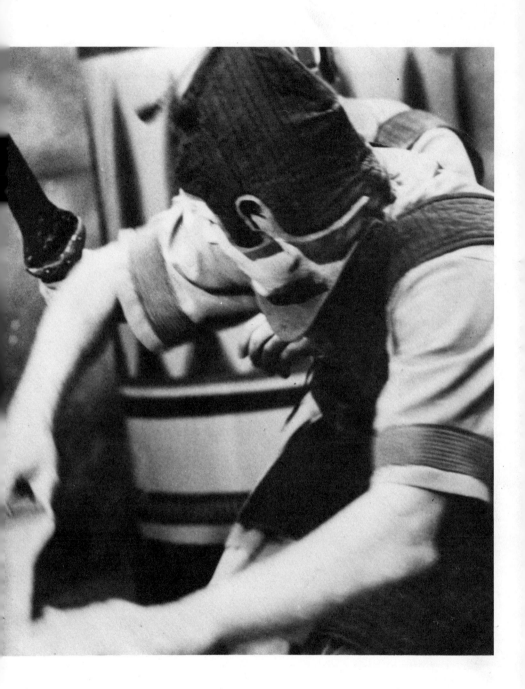

Bellamin killed him with the sword. Then he ran after Bentley and LaFarge.

Bentley lit the way with his flashlight. More guards chased them. LaFarge tripped and hit his head. He lay helpless as the first guard reached him. Bentley turned to help LaFarge. The flashlight beam swept onto the guard's face. The guard screamed with pain when the light hit his eyes. He dropped his sword and ran away.

It's the light!" Bentley yelled. "Their eyes can't stand the light!" He marched back toward the temple. All of the other guards fled when he turned the flashlight beam on them.

Bellamin and LaFarge followed Bentley back to the temple. Bellamin made LaFarge sit down and rest. Nearby, one of the Mole People popped out of the earth. The creature picked up the body of the dead guard.

Bentley turned on his flashlight. The Mole Man covered his eyes and escaped into his hole.

Suddenly, LaFarge jumped up. "We have to get away from them," he yelled. He ran back into the tunnel.

Bentley and Bellamin followed him. "LaFarge, wait," they called. But LaFarge was almost out of his mind. He ran blindly. His route led deeper into the earth.

LaFarge's legs finally gave out. When Bentley reached him, he heard a new noise up ahead. It sounded like the crack of a whip. Then came a low, inhuman scream.

Bentley and Bellamin crept forward. They turned a corner and stopped. Both men gasped in horror. Ahead lay a scene straight out of a nightmare.

■ ■ ■ ■ ■ ■ ■ ■ ■ ■ ■ ■ ■ ■ ■ ■ ■ ■ ■ ■

6.
A GIFT FROM SHARU

■ ■ ■ ■ ■ ■ ■ ■ ■ ■ ■ ■ ■ ■ ■ ■ ■ ■ ■ ■

In the dim light, Bentley saw dozens of Mole People. They were living in holes dug into the soft

The Sumerian guards patrol the area where the Mole People live.

earth. Whenever the Mole Men and Mole Women stood up, a Sumerian guard whipped them.

A guard entered with a large box of food. He threw food to the Mole People. The creatures fought for each handful. They were so hungry they'd do anything for a bite of food.

One piece of food rolled close to where the men were hiding. A Mole Man chased after the food. He roared with surprise when he saw the two men. Guards came to see what was going on.

Bentley wasn't worried. He pulled out his flashlight. Nothing happened! The switch was jammed.

The scientists turned back and pulled LaFarge to his feet. Then they ran for their lives. A mob of Sumerians and Mole People chased after them. At the last minute Bentley and the other men ducked into a side tunnel. The guards raced by without seeing them.

The three men stumbled deeper into the tunnel. Just as LaFarge was feeling safe, a Mole Man grabbed him. The creature had been hiding deep in the tunnel. His sharp claws ripped at LaFarge's face. Bentley clubbed the Mole Man with his flashlight. The shock freed the jammed switch. The light blazed into the Mole Man's eyes. He gave an animal cry of pain and ran away.

The rescue came too late. Huge claws had crushed LaFarge's head. Bentley and Bellamin pushed the body into a crack in the tunnel wall. They piled up

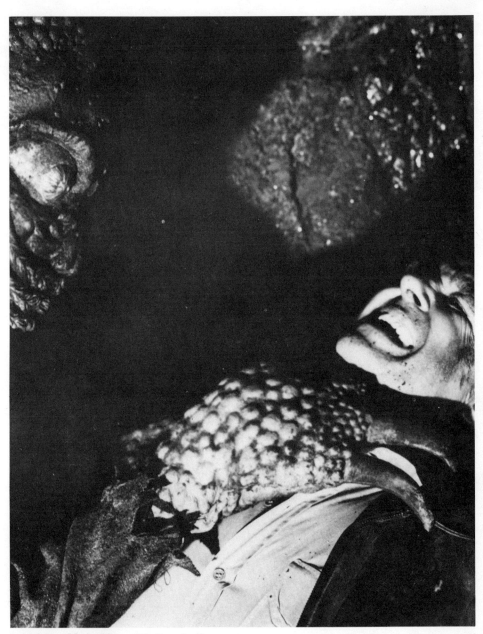

A hidden Mole Man catches LaFarge.

rocks to finish the job of burying their friend.

The men found their way back to the ruined temple. They had begun to fear that they wouldn't find an escape route.

As they rested, they heard Elinu's voice. "Do not use the Burning Light," the high priest begged. "The king now believes you are sent from the gods. He invites you to a royal feast."

Elinu led them to the palace. He wanted to know where LaFarge was. Bentley said that LaFarge had gone back to heaven.

King Sharu waited for them at a long stone table. "Now," Sharu asked. "Why did the Goddess send you here?"

"Ishtar sent us to learn of your needs," Bentley replied. "She wants to help you."

Sharu liked the answer. He called for dinner to be served. Servants brought in the food on stone dishes.

The king invites them to a feast.

"So that's it," Bellamin said as he tasted the food. "They live on mushrooms. It's one plant that can grow without light."

One of the serving girls caught Bentley's eye. She wasn't white-skinned and white-haired like the other Sumerians. Her hair was light brown, and her skin was like ivory.

The man's stare confused the girl. She dropped the plate she was holding. The accident made Sharu

Bentley's stare confused the girl. She didn't look like the other serving girls.

Bentley stops the guard from whipping the serving girl.

angry. He ordered a guard to whip her. Bentley jumped up, the flashlight in his hand. "I hold the Burning Light of Ishtar. This is the law!" he yelled.

Sharu raised his hand. "I will not defy the power of Ishtar," he said to Bentley. "Please sit down. Because you like Adad, I will give her to you. I cannot bear to look at her. Her skin and hair are much too dark. Old stories say all Sumerians looked like that long ago. I don't believe it."

Bentley didn't know what to say. Adad smiled at him and he felt himself blush. Sharu didn't notice his red face. The king was talking to Bellamin. Sharu said that sometimes too many babies were born. When that happened, some older people had to be sent to die in the fire of Ishtar.

A guard ran in with a message. A Mole Man had eaten the body of a dead guard. Sharu asked the guard if the guilty Mole Man had been found.

"Yes, we have him," the guard replied.

"Then kill him!" Sharu said. "We need the Beasts of the Dark to raise our food. We must keep them in our power."

7.
ELINU HATCHES A PLOT

After the meal, a servant led Bentley and Bellamin to a sleeping room. Bellamin was certain they'd never escape.

"Maybe the Mole People will help us," Bentley told him.

Bellamin looked sharply at his friend. "The Mole People won't help," he snapped. "They've been slaves too long. They were human once, but now they're worse than animals."

Adad came in with a pitcher of water. She also carried a lute so she could play soft music for Bentley. The graceful girl laid out white fur rugs for sleeping.

"You go to sleep, my lord," Adad said to Bentley. "I will watch over you while you dream."

Her soft voice pleased Bentley. He thought she was very beautiful. He wanted to protect her. "Adad, you must go back to your own family," he said. "You will be in danger if you stay."

Adad held on to Bentley's arm. "Don't make me go, lord! My home is now with you. The king said so."

Bentley tried to make her understand. "You are

free to go, or not to go," he said. "But I fear the high priest will send guards to harm us. If you're here, they may hurt you, too."

Adad didn't think anyone could defeat Bentley. She started playing her lute. "Tell me about your world, my lord," she said.

"In my world, there is light and color everywhere," Bentley told her. "The land is covered with growing things. The cities are filled with people like you and me."

"You are speaking of heaven!" Adad told him. Their eyes met and they smiled at each other.

Not far away, Elinu was speaking to the other

Elinu plots with the other priests for control.

priests. "The king believes the dark men are gods," he said. "But I say they are men, like you and I! They eat. They sleep. They show fear."

"That cannot be!" an old priest broke in. "They have the Burning Light. Only a god could have such power."

Elinu shook his head. "Not so! The power comes from the metal tube they carry. And think! If we had that tube, we could control the Mole People. We could even control the king!"

The priests smiled at the thought. Like Elinu, they didn't like taking orders from King Sharu.

Elinu knew he had won. He gave his orders. "Go where they go. Take the metal tube away from them. Bring it to me."

The next morning, Bentley and Bellamin set out to explore the tunnels. They didn't see the priest who followed them.

"Why don't we just give up?" Bellamin said bitterly. They had just reached another dead end.

"Because I don't like mushrooms!" Bentley laughed.

The two men sat down to rest. Bentley put the flashlight down. The priest crept closer and closer.

"Why don't you marry Adad? You could settle down here," Bellamin teased. "Just think, in another hundred years, archeologists will discover this world. But what a shock! All the little Sumerians will look like you!"

The priest was now hiding behind a rock just a few feet away. His fingers reached toward the magic tube. Bentley laughed at the joke and decided it was time to go on. He picked up the flashlight. As he stood up, the priest's hand closed on empty air.

■ ■

8.
BENTLEY FINDS
SOME ALLIES

■ ■

The Sumerians raised small, white-haired goats. Armed guards watched the goats carefully. They were worth more than gold.

Some Mole Men entered the goat's cavern from a side tunnel. They carried heavy sacks of mushrooms. The Mole Men were tired and hungry. They dropped the mushrooms into feeding bins. The goats were better fed than the Mole Men.

"The Mole Men are getting weak," one guard said. "Shall we feed them?"

"No!" their captain ordered.

Just then Bentley and Bellamin walked into the cavern. The guards all turned to watch them. One of the Mole Men saw his chance. He stuffed some mushrooms into his mouth. He wasn't quick enough. The captain saw what he had done.

The Mole Man is afriad of the guards.

"Guards! Give that beast sixty lashes!" he called.

The guards whipped the creature until he fell down. Bentley couldn't stand it. "Stop!" he called. "The Mole Man was hungry."

"My job is to keep them that way," the captain replied coldly. "They're easier to control when they're hungry."

While they talked, the Mole Man crept away. He slipped into one of the tunnels. The captain drew his knife and ran after him. Far into the tunnel, the captain suddenly sank into a hole. Sharp claws reached up and pulled him down into the earth. The Mole People were learning to fight back against the cruel guards.

When the captain didn't return, the archeologists

went back to their sleeping room. They found Adad there, playing her lute.

"You are beautiful, Adad," Bentley told her.

"No, I am ugly," the girl said. "The priests say so."

"Believe me, you are not ugly," Bentley said. He held her hand. "If I can find a way out of here, will you go with me?"

"To the land of light and colors?" Adad asked. "Yes! If my eyes will work in your world, I will go with you gladly."

Bentley told Adad that her eyes were just like his own. As he put his arms around her, a priest came into the room. "The king wishes to see you at once!" the priest told the two men.

Sharu and Elinu were upset. They had just learned of the captain's death. Sharu asked Bentley to use the flashlight to bring the Mole People under control.

Bentley refused. "We will not help you punish your slaves," Bentley said. He nodded to Bellamin and they left.

Elinu was so angry he could hardly speak. "See! They are against us. Take away the magic tube and they will be helpless."

Sharu shook his head. "No, we must not defy Ishtar. Guards! Arrest three Mole Men. Whip them until they are dead. That will show them we still have power over them."

The guards dragged three Mole Men to the prison cell. They chained the creatures to the wall. As a guard lifted his whip, a beam of light blinded him. Bentley and Bellamin had followed them. Other guards ran in, but the flashlight forced them back.

Then the light faded and went out. Bentley shook the flashlight. Nothing happened. The batteries were dead. "We're safe as long as the guards think we have the light," he told Bellamin.

The two men freed the Mole Men from their chains. "Go!" Bentley said. He pointed to the sliding door.

One Mole Man stopped in front of them. His strange eyes glowed. "We re-mem-ber," he said. Then he left the cell.

Bentley and Bellamin looked at each other. "They're still human!" Bentley said. "Maybe they can help us find a way out!"

■ ■ ■ ■ ■ ■ ■ ■ ■ ■ ■ ■ ■ ■ ■ ■ ■ ■ ■ ■

9.
A DEADLY MEAL

■ ■ ■ ■ ■ ■ ■ ■ ■ ■ ■ ■ ■ ■ ■ ■ ■ ■ ■ ■

King Sharu called Elinu and other Sumerian leaders to a meeting. "Ishtar has turned her face away from us," Sharu said. "The beasts are not growing enough food."

"It is the fault of the strangers!" Elinu shouted. "Because of them, the Mole People disobey us."

Sharu had already made up his mind. "There is no choice. The law is clear. Some of us must die in the Room of Light. Only then will Ishtar send food for all."

The word went out to all the people. They filled the area in front of the temple. Sharu sat on his throne, with Elinu beside him. A pretty, white-skinned girl stepped forward. Slow, sad music played. The girl danced in front of a huge, stone door.

The dance ended. Elinu called for the victims who would die for Ishtar. Guards led a group of men and women toward the door. Elinu and the other priests put pieces of cloth over their own heads. Everyone else just closed their eyes.

Then Elinu pulled a lever. The stone door opened slowly. A flood of bright light poured into the cavern. One by one, the victims stepped into the Room of Light. The door closed behind them, cutting off their cries of pain. At a signal from Elinu, everyone left the area.

Later, the priests returned. When the door opened, the Room of Light was dark. The Eye of Ishtar no longer burned. The priests carried out the dead bodies. They were all burned black.

An officer of the guards hurried up to Elinu. He took the high priest to see a bundle carried by two

Elinu uncovers the face of the dead LaFarge.

other guards. Elinu pulled back the top cover. LaFarge's dead face stared up at him. A look of victory lit up Elinu's face. He sent for King Sharu.

"They said he was in heaven," Elinu told the king. "But look! He was only a man, as we are men. We must strike the others quickly, before they destroy us all!"

Sharu knew now that he had been tricked. He almost choked on his anger. "You are free to act," he told Elinu. "Destroy them!"

Bentley and Bellamin did not know that LaFarge's body had been found. They were sitting in their bedroom when Adad came in. She brought large plates of food. The men were hungry. The mushrooms didn't taste good, but they ate them anyway.

The men began to feel sleepy. Bellamin dropped his spoon and fell forward on the table. Bentley fought to keep his eyes open. Someone had put a sleeping drug in the mushrooms! He saw shock and surprise on Adad's face. That made him feel better. At least she wasn't part of the plan to drug them.

Elinu and his guards ran into the bedroom. Bentley tried to fight, but he was too weak. The guards tied up the two men and took them away. Adad hid in a corner. No one noticed her.

The high priest picked up the flashlight and hid it in his robes. "Now, I have the power!" Elinu cried out. No one had ever told him about dead batteries.

Bellamin and Bentley lay tied side by side as a girl does the Dance of Death.

10.
BEHIND THE DOORS
OF DEATH

Bentley woke up slowly. His head hurt. He tried to move, but his hands were tied. Bellamin lay beside him, tied up just as tightly. The door to the Room of Light rose above them.

Drums beat slowly. Elinu stepped forward. Bentley believed he was about to die. He looked for Adad, but she wasn't there.

Adad was far away. She was headed toward the home of the Mole People. Whenever she saw a guard, she hid. Finally, a guard saw her. She started running. The guard shouted and chased her.

Just then, a Mole Man reached up and pulled Adad into his hole. Other Mole People quickly buried themselves in the earth. When the guard arrived, everything was quiet.

Back at the temple, strong arms picked up Bentley and Bellamin. Elinu pulled the lever to open the door. Guards carried the men into the blinding light. The guards backed out and the door closed.

Guards drag Bentley and Bellamin into the Eye of Ishtar.

"The will of Ishtar has been done," Elinu said in a loud voice. The people bowed their heads. As they did so, hundreds of Mole People cut through the walls of the cavern. The Sumerians screamed and ran in all directions.

More Mole People came out of the walls. Elinu pulled the magic tube out of his robes. He pushed the button, but no light flashed on. A Mole Man picked up the high priest and threw him across the temple floor. Another Mole Man threw himself on Sharu.

Adad ran to the great door. She pulled at the lever, but couldn't move it. Behind her, the last guards fled. Sharu and Elinu were dead. Adad hammered at the door with her fists. Tears ran down her cheeks. She was sure Bentley was dying.

The Mole People came to help her. They pushed against the heavy door. Finally, the door crashed to the ground. Blazing light filled the cavern. The Mole People staggered away, leaving Adad alone. She was afraid, but she didn't want to live without Bentley. She closed her eyes against the light and walked into the chamber.

Bentley and Bellamin were waiting for her, unharmed. Bentley held Adad close for a long time. Then he pointed upward. The bright light came from a V-shaped crack in the rock. "To your people, that light was the Eye of Ishtar. It meant death by burning," Bentley said. "But to us, it means life."

The light felt warm on Adad's skin. Slowly, she

opened her eyes. "I can see! It's not too bright! I'm going to like it in your world," she said in an excited voice. "But what about the Mole People? We can't leave them here."

"The light is deadly for them," Bentley said. "I'm afraid they will have to live in darkness forever."

It was a hard climb up the V-shaped crack. Finally they reached the open air. Light was everywhere. It sparkled on the new snow. Adad held out her arms. "Your world is more beautiful than any dream," she said.

The air was cold. They hurried back to the ruined temple. Their backpacks lay where they had left them. Bentley helped Adad put on warm clothing.

Suddenly the ground began to move. An earthquake shook Kuh-i-Tara like a dog shakes a rat. Deep within the mountain, the entire roof of the cavern fell in. Sharu's lost world soon lay buried under tons of rock.

The earthquake also sent a snowbank sliding downward. A mass of snow pulled Adad away from Bentley. She was completely covered up. Bentley and Bellamin dug like madmen to find her.

Bentley uncovered her face. She was barely breathing. He started giving her first aid. At last, her eyes opened. In a little while she was strong enough to start the climb downward.

Bentley led the way. Just before they reached the base camp, he had a terrible thought. Except for

Adad is rescued.

Adad, he didn't have any proof of his great find.

"Someday, I'll dig up what's left of Sharu's world," he said.

"No, please don't," Adad begged. "Let the mountain keep its secrets."

Bentley sighed, but agreed to do as Adad wished. After all, there were plenty of other places he could dig.

Besides, who would believe his story?